For my mother, who is very much alive.

Published by Stanchion Books, LLC

StanchionZine.com

Edited by Katie Schmeling

Cover art by Jeff Bogle

ISBN: 979-8-88862-256-8

Ghost Mom

T Guzman

STANCHION

Table of Contents

Part 1: Death

Ghost Mom

When your mother dies, she comes back as a ghost. You find her late one night—as she was a night owl in the same way that you are a night owl—sitting on the couch. Curled up in a quilt. Eating day-old popcorn. Watching Shirley Temple movies. Her hair no longer in rollers or done up in the way your mother always had her hair in rollers or done up, but flat pulled to one side—her figure translucent white with a slight shimmer. You want to say, what are you doing here? Aren't you supposed to be dead? Is this a trick? Hello? I missed you.

But you don't say any of these words.

Because two people, who are loud and can't stand to go unheard, have a quiet relationship.

Instead, you say, have you been well?

You sit down. The ghost of your mother passes you the popcorn. It's late. You have work tomorrow, but the movie's almost over. You can feel the denouement coming through the black and white, the tension growing ever taut. You stay. Watch as everything turns out alright in the end, and Shirley goes into her final number, tapping first up some stairs then down some stairs then out and into the brilliant sunlight. Her voice angelic. Her curls radiant. All dimples and beaming at the camera. Savoring the moment

before the orchestra swells, pronouncing the
end, and the fade to black.

Anything at All

After your mother dies, everyone keeps telling you if you need anything, anything at all, all you need is ask. What you need right now—could honestly go for more than anything else—is candy. A Ho-Ho or Ding Dong. Rice crispy treats. Pizza. Someone to take a look at your car cause it's old, and it makes a funny noise, and you don't have the money, especially now, to have someone look at it, but also you're terrified to have someone look at your car 'cause what if your car—like your mother just a week ago—is dying and wouldn't that just be the luck! Someone to pay off your student loans. Or get your landlord to fix the water heater so you can take a shower at a reasonable temperature. Perhaps, they could come over and give your neighbors a piece of their mind. Get them to stop throwing parties every weekend, or at least invite you to the parties they throw every weekend so you have something to do other than listen to a bunch of people have a good time while you sit around not having a good time. That—and you know this is the most absurd ask of all of your asks—on those nights when you wake up and it's past midnight—all stores closed, not a single gas station open, the world seeming abandoned, devoid of all humanity—

and you are inexplicably struck with the overwhelming urge to eat a Snickers bar even though you have never been the kind of person who eats Snickers bars, and it appears as if any and all hope of obtaining a Snickers bar is naught, that they make the impossible possible.

Or maybe they know somebody kind.

Someone who drinks tea instead of coffee. Goes for bike rides instead of runs. Enjoys the quiet. Spreads out in the sun with a book and can't stop humming a tune they can't quite recall but can't forget. Dependable. Who don't yell or scream. Won't go amorphous on you and float away. Solid enough to hold you. To occasionally snore so loud that it wakes you when you sleep and you in between the waking and sleeping world are reminded—having forgotten for the briefest of seconds—that, yes, there is someone here always beside you.

But you're being stupid.

That's not what they meant. You know that.

So you say, thank you. If you can think of anything, anything at all, you'll be sure to let them know.

Ghost Mom II

It's been a long day, and when you get home, you fall asleep without eating or watching TV or even undressing—such the raucous life you live now that you're an adult and on your own. When you wake up, it's two a.m. You're starving and a bit dehydrated. You walk into the living room on the way to the kitchen only to find the ethereal specter of your mother sitting on the couch watching *Seven Brides for Seven Brothers*. Your mother's supposed to be dead in heaven or reincarnated or in the nothingness you suspect death just might be. Yet, here she is the fifth time this week, watching all the shows she watched from before she was dead. You ask her if this is how she imagined her death would be? If she wouldn't, perhaps, like to be getting out there more and enjoying the death that she has? She asks if you wouldn't also like to be getting out there more? Suggests maybe you shouldn't be spending so much time talking to your ghost mom, watching old musicals.

Touché.

You walk to the kitchen to make grilled cheese with tortillas the way your mom did when she was a living mother and not the ghost mom she has become. Not out of some sadness or nostalgia or attempt to make some emotional connection to the past. This is all the energy you have in you, like how this was all the energy your mother had when she was off her second shift between her third. Sustenance with plenty of butter. From the living room, you can hear the seven brothers and the girls they've just kidnapped. The quiet as they make their way through the snow pass. The only sound the hooves of horses that take the girls to their winter prison. The screams that come after they are through, beyond reach. The snow crashing down. The girls, voices but a whimper now, realizing they have no chance to escape or be rescued for quite some time.

How to Get a Ghost Mom

First, your mother needs to die.

And it'll be a whole thing with a eulogy and a funeral and a few people making complete asses of themselves—*thank god* it isn't you making a complete ass of yourself—and in all these moments you wonder, how to find the time to feel anything?

So, you don't feel anything.

Or maybe you feel everything.

Perhaps, you don't really know how to feel.

Are certain you feel every way simultaneously despite this being impossible.

So you have a séance.

Buy a crystal ball, some incense. Burn a candle.

Write letters to your dead mom. At midnight standing over their grave—the moon in waning gibbous—burn these letters. Let the ash drift to who knows where. It's dark and windy and cold. You're just in a t-shirt and jeans. Didn't bring a jacket. Tsk, tsk. Honestly that more than anything is likely to get your mom up and out of their grave.

Or maybe consult a medium.

A medium with string beads for doors 'cause in all the stories good mediums have string beads for doors. But don't spend a lot of money cause mediums are scams—you know it—and having a pretend ghost mom instead of an actual ghost mom can be preferable. Your pretend ghost mom is probably kinder. All the complicated emotions that are normal between any parent and their child aren't problems with a pretend ghost mom. Unless you want or need them to be.

Really though, demons are more reliable. You could make a pact with a demon. Ask them, offering up the souls of your dead mother's enemies, to traverse the land of the dead and bring them back. This is hard so you might find that your demon, who perhaps isn't as reliable as you'd hoped, isn't up to the challenge of a full resurrection. The land of the dead is not exactly a picnic after all. Then you might suggest possession. Demons know all about possession, and while you can probably convince the demon to place the soul of your dead mother into a human body—again an enemy or nemesis in mind would be handy—it's going to be easier, and more convenient, to have said demon put your mother's soul into a household object. A doll is a classic for a reason.

But you can't deny the perverse pleasure—a reminder that even the most stable parent and child relationship is fraught—of putting your dead mom's soul into something more peculiar. A television? Paperweight? Maybe a snow globe! A camera so that they can always be in every picture? A book is underappreciated and very classy. But perhaps you are thinking this is too glib. Remember your ghost mom in whatever form they take will always be an individual choice and reflection of you and your mother's relationship before their untimely demise.

You can always do nothing.

Go about your day. Walk to the mailbox. See if there is any mail though there is never any mail 'cause no one writes letters in this day and age. Still, it gets you out the house and that isn't nothing. Or so you tell yourself. You could— probably should—go to the grocery store. Buy food. Make the food that you bought into something edible. It doesn't need to be good. Edible is enough. It won't matter to you all that much considering everything. So, eat your food. Take a shower. Brush your teeth. Turn off all the lights in your house and go to bed.

Sleep or don't sleep.

Think about your mother or don't think about your mother. It's all the same.

And look at that, the sun has come up.

The next day arrives regardless of whether you want it to.

Start the day anew.

Only on this day, walk a bit further than the mailbox—once around the block for the sun. And the day after that, maybe go to your mother's grave? Or you know, maybe don't do that. You could visit friends and avoid talking about anything, enjoying the sound of voices that are not your own. You could go to the movies. Make plans with your significant other that you may or may not keep, but in the planning stage nod to yourself in feeling as if you've made some marked progress even if you don't, and likely won't, keep said plans.

But perhaps, your mother—in their living life—loved making plans. Maybe your mother was an avid movie goer. Going to the matinees alone, getting full on popcorn, ruining dinner. Visiting and laughing with friends, significant others. Enjoyed the feeling of walking over the threshold of a front door and into the heat of the afternoon—everything suddenly blinding in the sun, skin warming, the air thick with humidity and the potential of evening just around the corner.

Well, you can always do different things.

Mindless activities to make the days feel smaller.

The world has no shortage of things to do and places to avoid.

And voila, look at that, now you have yourself a ghost mom.

Ghost Party

You wake up to the sound of disco funk coming from downstairs, and so you charge down into the living room and see all your dinnerware going mad around the room—forks and knives shimming and strutting across your counter top, plates up in the air bobbing to the beat, pots and pans in sync soaring across the ceiling, the toaster leading a contingent of appliances in some sort of dance that you can't be certain but suspect is the hustle—and in the center of it all, your ghost mom, her eyes closed, swaying to the groove, and you are one part in awe of this otherworldly chaos and one part terrified and incensed about the state of your apartment and the prospect of getting your deposit back, and so you slam your hand down on the turntable, and the needle skips down into the gutter and the music stops, and all your housewares freeze, and you cringe expecting the fall—all your things soon to be shattered on the floor—but instead they hang there in motionless silence, and so you ask your ghost mom, what the hell is going on!

She says, nothing.

You say you can see that this—whatever this is—is not nothing.

Your ghost mom shrugs, floats to the ground. Your mismatched plates and dull spoons and out of date appliances flutter to the ground with her.

She says, what? Ghosts can dance, can't they!

You say, you can most certainly see that.

Then it occurs to you that she used the word *ghosts* as in plural. You realize that while you can see your ghost mom, and you know there are other ghosts in this world, that your ghost mom is not the only ghost in existence, you cannot see these other ghosts. Have no way of knowing just how many ghosts are here or have been here or always been here, and suddenly it feels very cold, and you're glancing about at your toaster and microwave and silverware with newfound suspicion.

What do you mean by ghosts, you say.

She says, what, with a particularly annoying disinterest.

You say, don't what me, what do you mean by the word *ghosts*.

She says, what do you think I'm just throwing some kind of ghost party here?

You scream, having rarely ever screamed at your living mother let alone your dead one, that yes that is exactly what you think, that she's having some kind of ghost party in the middle of the goddamn night when she well knows that you have work tomorrow, and unlike her, have things to do, a life—a living one—that needs tending to, and once you've let everything out— all these grievances you've barely allowed yourself to acknowledge—you immediately regret the words you've said, but know it's too late.

She says, oh. That she doesn't even know any other ghosts so you shouldn't worry.

You don't say anything.

She says, sorry.

The needle from the turntable loops in the gutter, popping and clicking, going nowhere and playing nothing. You settle in on the couch next to a whisk that moments before had been doing cartwheels—end on end—across your walls. You say that it must be hard being dead and everything. That it can't be easy giving up all the things you once had before. You say you're sorry about blowing up. You didn't mean what you said before. That if she wants to have a dance party, she can have a dance party. Your ghost mom can break anything she wants, really, you don't mind. You say you're sorry she's dead. That you don't want her to be dead. Except you don't actually say any of these words.

All you can say is, it's okay.

Your Ghost Mom Visits You at the Grocery Store

You are surprised to learn your ghost mom isn't tethered to only your house when she walks up to you in Walmart at three in the morning. She tells you that she haunts many places. That the door man here always talked down to her like she couldn't speak English all the while trying to look down her blouse, and so now, she's giving him kidney stones for the trouble. Your ghost mom tells you that there is a power in death, time is infinite, and her list is long.

She says this as if it's nothing. Like this past grievance is a minor humiliation on a list of humiliations and all of this is mere formality. You suppose it is. You want to say something, tell your ghost mom that she can rest easy now. Move on from this horrid world. That she can entrust these vengeances to you, but you know that you are just as powerless now as you were when you were a child. And so, you go to apologize for all the things you cannot correct, but your ghost mom has gone up the aisle pointing out a sale on bell peppers, eyeing the avocados, explaining for the hundredth time how to pick the perfect one, reminding you that tomatillos are in season right now.

Ghost Mom III

Your ghost mom's around so much you begin to forget your ghost mom is in fact a ghost mom and not a regular living one, so that when a 70s Singing Legend dies, you go to first call your mom then remember she's dead then realize that surely she must already know being dead and all. That her connection to the cosmos must now be far beyond the occasional premonition she had in her living life.

So, you close your phone. Take off your shoes and put away all your work things, beginning the transition from your public form to your private one.

You turn on the TV.

Avoid thinking about how hungry you are.

Stare at the television and wonder if perhaps all people that die become ghosts.

That the 70s Singing Legend is now a ghost and somewhere out there in the infinite is an old abandoned discoteca—aged and faded but otherwise uncorrupted. That ghosts at this moment are gathering there. Souls lured in by bass and falsetto. Vague shapes under the neon afterglow. That right now the 70s Singing Legend is taking the stage exalted by a raucous chorus of ghostly howls. Playing out all the hits. The groove is smooth, and the house is on fire, and the ghost of your mother is there—back row in the shadows—raptured in that teenage crush kind of way that never leaves you. Even in death.

The disco ball turns.

And everything glimmers and shines.

And 70s Singing Legend is at his end, taking his bow, existing stage left.

For the living, the night would end here. People would get in their cars. Drive to their homes and lay in bed, their bodies hot and beating to the pulse of songs still remembered in every fiber of their muscles as they drift off to sleep in their warm beds, shared or empty.

But here—in the Afterlife—everyone is dead. The sun never rises. The night never ends and another band takes his place. It starts again. The neon never fading. And the 70s Singing Legend, newly deceased, takes a step back from it all. Stands next the ghost of your mother. He smiles a *Tiger Beat* smile. Says to her, so this is death? She nods and he tilts his head back with a grin that belongs taped to back of locker doors. He looks over at her. Looks over at the dance floor, filled with phantoms of the night who have no other place they'd rather be than here and now. He holds out a hand to her.

Asks, would you like this dance?

Part II: Afterlife

Afterlife

Your ghost mom's curled up on the couch with a box of tissues, watching *Somewhere in Time* for the fourth time this week when you tell her she needs to get out more. She looks up at you with ghost tears—shards of transparent blue that pierce the dark—and says she will when you will, so you both make a pact to try harder.

You go on a date.

It's not a very good date. The restaurant is old and all the employees look depressed, which you find oddly comforting. It's clear your date isn't impressed. You can tell she's resisting the urge to look at her phone, which you can't hold against her. You aren't very good at talking, and your date ends up doing all the talking except she doesn't like doing all the talking. Who would? So, you try talking more so as to not be a bad date, and start telling your date about your ghost mom. As soon as the words leave your mouth, you realize you've made a mistake. But once you've started, there's no way to stop. You tell your date about how your ghost mom's always watching classic cinema on your TV, haunting all the people who have wronged her, staring out the window, making all the babies cry as they pass by with their mothers. You tell your date how you wish your ghost mom would get out more, start enjoying her afterlife, and let you begin yours. But you have trouble expressing these things 'cause you know how fortunate you are to have a ghost mom. How so many people would be ecstatic to have their mother, even in ghost form, back for even just a few hours. How sometimes you find it hard to even go home knowing that she's likely to be there. You tell your date, you aren't a fool either, though. You understand that ghost moms, like living moms, can't last forever. That surely this can't last forever.

Your date says, hmmm, nods, and sips from her iced tea till it is nearly empty.

The food arrives.

You both politely eat and forgo conversation altogether. You stare down at your plate. Your date does the same. The restaurant picks up and fills with the cacophony of people talking and laughing with and over each other. The awkwardness is killing you. But still, you can't help enjoying the quiet company, the noise of somewhere that isn't your apartment. Part of you can't wait till this is over and done with, and part of you dreads the end hurriedly rushing towards you.

Outside, the date officially at its end, you apologize. Your date says you don't need to apologize, but you both do in fact know you need to apologize, so you apologize again. Your date says it's okay. You say thanks because you don't know what else to say. Then you stand there as people move between you and your date, coming and going towards some unknown destination. You don't even dare inquire about another date, and say nothing, so your date walks away and so you walk away.

The streets are busy.

But sometimes walking alone along with a dense crowd can feel like you are not alone but a part of some collective movement headed towards somewhere exciting even when you're simply going down the block to the corner store for soda and a snack. This is what you loved about living in a city when you moved here years ago. But now it feels incredibly lonely to be among the busy—couples and families and twenty somethings, hustling off to fulfill some urgent purpose or seek some pleasure or comfort or condolence.

And as you revel in melancholy, you wonder about all the ghosts.

Not just your ghost mom.

That this city must be full of them sight unseen.

Ghosts sitting at the streetside tables of cafes, wandering among the pumps at the gas station, in restaurants, in bars, trying to catch the attention of servers that will never come, floating down the street eavesdropping on conversations, enjoying the occasional busker at the crosswalks.

You find yourself in a park as dusk settles into evening. All the streetlights blink on in bunches down the line. The park is empty. It's one of those small out of the way parks used by locals. You sit on a park bench and feel as if you are suddenly heartbroken. It's an odd feeling to have, but you are quite certain you are crushed. It is only a failed date, you tell yourself. There will be other chances. Other dates. Future loves and friends. Trips and companionship. Adventures unforeseen. Gloom—you must convince yourself—must only be endured for a short time. Yet you cannot shake the desolation. The dread of the evening. This year that seems to go on for an eternity. These urges you find at the oddest times to flee, to seek refuge, as if a threat were upon your life. But where to go? What to escape?

None of it makes sense.

The sun sets, and you sit under the orange tinge of street lights.

You are not alone, or so you consider. Surely, this place too must be full of ghosts beyond your sight somewhere in the hinterlands. And for a second, you will yourself into believing that you can see them. Ghost families huddled just over there around a picnic table—balloons and silly hats—celebrating some birthday, or perhaps some death. A phantom teen on their cellphone off to the side above it all, flipping through feeds of lives they can only see at a distance now. The ghastly wails of child apparitions chasing after one another, playing some game that will never end. Ghost dads, or perhaps a ghost older brother, pushing the spectral figure of a toddler at the swing set.

It's a comforting delusion, all these ghosts.

To know that when something ends, it doesn't just end.

But you aren't a fool, and so you prepare yourself to leave. To go home to find that your ghost mother may or may not be there. You are not certain which you want. Immobilized between the terror of both guilt and grief. Struck as if possessed by sorrow. But then there is a rustle in the trees just behind you. You turn your head and despite your dejection, you feel relieved. A glimmer. Maybe, there is still a turn yet in this evening, a promise of the unexpected? You rise from your seat, spirits lifted, an effervescence about you, and round yourself to meet whatever phantoms will appear!

The sound emerges.

But it is no ghost or specter, living or deceased.

It is only the face of a raccoon that greets you. Come out now that the sun has dipped below the horizon to find all that is discarded. You sigh, feeling utterly foolish. Turn your back to the furry creature that has gone about climbing the nearest trash bin, and you begin the long walk home. The raccoon unaware of your existence, only ever looking up briefly as you pass by.

Ghost Moms' Support Group

Your ghost mom appears one morning in your kitchen just after you've woken and gone about making your Sunday eggs, which are eggs that you make every Sunday and aren't particularly special or unique except to you. Apparently, your ghost mom's been going to a ghost moms' support group for the newly deceased.

She tells you that this ghost moms' support group is made up of a bunch of weirdos. Ghost moms that go around following their loved ones all the time, looking in on them, chronicling the life that comes after their own, lives they can't be a part of. She tells you most of them—the ghost moms—can't even communicate with their living loved ones. That all they are doing is haunting their kids and spouses. Letting their *presence* be known by pushing tea cups off the tops of coffee tables, closing and opening doors when no one else is around, making curtains flutter, creaks in wooden floors and staircases, scaring the shit out of cats and making dogs go bonkers.

You say, but surely they must talk about other things, too? That it must be good to talk to someone. That being dead must be difficult.

Maybe moving on, you tell your ghost mom, wouldn't be such a bad thing.

Your mother in her living life was never one for therapy.

Like your mother, you've never been to therapy even though you are well aware you should definitely go to therapy, so this turn of events surprises you, but you want to be supportive.

Outside, the birds are chirping like mad. Dawn is turning into morning, and the sun is coming in through the kitchen window giving everything a burned look of orange glow. You're moving the eggs around by way of moving the pan around. You aren't much of a cook, but this Sunday morning routine brings you solace, and you are getting into it, going inward into that distant place you've always gone when you're really into something, stripping away the physical world around you till everything is quiet, comfortable. So, you move down and check the sausages you got going in the oven. Shift to the side and set up the toast. Open the fridge and select the right kind of jam, inspecting each one with careful consideration, which, given this morning light, you've decided is apricot. You put water in the kettle. Select mint tea. Five minutes left, you figure. Just a flip of the eggs, and perfection in breakfast form.

A shift in the air.

A door slams from the other room.

You look up, snapped back to this place and time.

Your ghost mom asks you if she was a good mother?

You ask what's brought about this question?

Turn your attention back to the eggs—the flip having gone all wrong—the yolks broken in your distraction.

Your ghost mom says that's not an answer.

And she's right that's not an answer.

Ghost Life
Part I

Your ghost mom is starting to make a ghost life for herself. You see her less and less as of late, and when she is around all she does is talk about all the things she's been up to while you have been up to exactly jack and shit.

She asks you if you knew there's an all-ghost rugby league?

You say, no you didn't know that.

It's your day off, and you're at the park. You figured the sun and open air would do you some good, and at least give you the illusion as if you live an interesting life, so here you are, laying on a blanket, your head facing towards the sun, listening to the kids playing over by the jungle gym, parents talking gossip and weekend plans and for the most part talking about nothing.

Your ghost mom says, they play on Sundays here in the park, the ghost ruby league. And by here she means the open field that you're currently lying in. Sometimes, she says, they even play at the same time as the living rugby league. That when these two overlap, it's a sight to be seen. The living rugby players constantly shivering, fumbling the ball, as all the ghost players glide through their living bodies as they move down the pitch. How when ghost bodies collide it's like lightning erupting between clouds—a blinding flash then thunder.

You close your eyes as your face grows warmer and try to imagine the scene. A ghost stand where you lay right now of specter spectators, cheering on as their team wins or loses or scores or touchdowns or whatever it is that happens in rugby since you are fairly ignorant on the subject.

They call it a pitch, your ghost mom says, did you know that?

No, you didn't but you wish you could see it, you say, keeping your eyes closed tight.

And she says, no you don't, not really 'cause then you'd have to be dead.

Ghost Life
Part II

Your life is a ghost story albeit not a very scary one.

Still, you find this hard to explain.

Late over drinks with a friend that you haven't seen in ages, you tell your friend that your dead mom, who is no longer living—a thing you neglected to inform her about—is now a ghost mom. And being a ghost, it's true that she's transparent, can turn on TVs and mess with electronics, but isn't actually all that scary.

She doesn't write things on mirrors.

Or recreate grisly scenes of blood and gore.

She isn't even good at making spooky wails, either.

And this, you tell your friend, who is beginning to seem more and more disinterested, makes no sense since your mother was quite the singer when she was alive and could wail like a banshee. You tell your friend about how your ghost mom mostly just pops back into your life whenever she feels like it without any real consideration for you. How you'll be putting away the groceries and all of a sudden you hear an ethereal voice behind you telling you not to put the milk in the fridge door 'cause it'll just spoil quicker, which you guess isn't all the different from when she was a living mom.

Your friend looks out the window as people come and go and meet with friends and more than friends. She asks why you asked her out tonight, looking like she expected something else.

You say to talk 'cause it's been forever.

She doesn't say much. The two of you just drink beers and talk about nothing.

You consider that this is an odd reaction to the news of your ghost mom though you're not sure what it is that you expected.

Warmth

Your ghost mom doesn't much care for the décor in your apartment. Notices the bare walls, lack of human touches beside old furniture, a second-hand coffee table, and half-empty bookshelves —all from differing decades and motifs. Your ghost mom says she may be a ghost, but even to her, this place feels cold. She says that it lacks warmth.

Perhaps a plant?

Something to put on the bookshelves, your ghost mom suggests.

And so you tell her about all the plants you had before. The menagerie of flora and fauna you inherited upon her death after the funeral. Bouquets of penny picotees and tulips. Roses and carnations of all colors. Exquisite orchids. Bamboo and sunflowers. Tiny fruit trees of oranges and lemons. Weeping figs. Deep red poppies so vivid they hurt the eyes to see. Daisies and peonies mixed pink and white surrounded by baby's breath. And ferns. The ferns! Ferns as far as the eye can see! So many damned ferns that you couldn't make it from the living room to the kitchen without tripping over one! Fronds clogging up vacuum after vacuum!

A cactus with a single magenta flower askew on the top.

Fuzzy as if begging to be touched on the windowsill.

You tell your ghost mom to imagine it. The white walls, so plain now, garish with life and color, ivy dripping down the walls. The delight of pollen and the scent of wilting petals. Gnats assailing you every time you open the door.

A botanical paradise, you say!

Your apartment so humid and earthy it was like death for anyone with allergies.

How you don't exactly have a green thumb, so you ended up hauling out plant after plant for weeks and months, desiccated, colors subdued and drawn out, to the dumpster. The bookshelves emptying. Walls returning to their beige white blandness. That your plant ineptitude truly knows no bounds! That though they were the last to go, you even managed to kill the bamboo and cactus, which in hindsight you are pretty sure had more to do with pressure and over attention than anything else.

No. You don't do plants. Honestly, you rather your apartment stays barren.

That you can live with cold.

Ghost Friend

Your ghost mom's been making some ghost friends, so she doesn't come around as much. This of course you are happy about. You don't want your ghost mom to become a homebody. You are glad she is getting out there, meeting people, albeit dead ones.

You do not wish to be morbid, so you'd never told your mother before, but you often imagined the life your mother would've had, had she not had you. You drew pictures in your mind of her standing center stage, jean jacket, mic in hand, a crowd that reached out to be even an inch closer. On trains to spontaneous destinations across Europe, departing with some boy she'd just met and couldn't yet bear to part with. Postcards and patches of states and parks and scenic views in glove boxes and sewn on backpacks. Your mother with an easel, secluded in a cabin. Riding a motorcycle in Montana. A moped in France. Hair long and braided. Short and dyed vivid blue. An endless universe of mothers who didn't have to turn down opportunities or worry themselves sick or work three shifts and sleep through Sundays to make it through the next week.

You of course are not wishing that you were never born.

You are glad to be alive even when being alive is difficult.

Your ghost mom is over today. She's at the window staring down at the neighborhood cats and making them go wild, giving little kids that pass by frights as she has taken to doing whenever she comes to visit. She tells you about a particular ghost friend she's made. He's an artist, she says. That her ghost friend used to— when he was very much alive—paint these detailed portraits of old buildings. Yes, that's right, your ghost mom says, portraits. She says you'd probably like them. You can't deny that these portraits sound like something you'd like. That even the pretentiousness of calling paintings of buildings portraits appeals to you. You wonder if your ghost mom and this ghost friend are more than ghost friends. If your ghost mom is buttering you up to meet him. That she is asking for your approval of her other worldly activities. You wonder if you'll actually even be able to see this ghost friend, since you do not possess the sight and cannot see all ghosts but just your ghost mom. And at this point in all this thinking, you realize you've lost the thread of what your ghost mom has been saying.

You ask if she could repeat that one more time.

She says, she's thinking of taking classes at the local community college where her ghost friend used to teach in his living life.

You tell her this is a great idea!

Your mother, in her living life, was always smarter than she was ever given the opportunity to show. You once asked your mother why she had you. You were a kid, and even as a kid you knew your mother was pro-choice and so the option was there. Yet you exist. Your mother—at this time very much alive—said that it was simple, that she could just feel it. Feel that she wanted to have you. You never know if you should believe this simple explanation. You suspect there were a myriad of cultural pressures and fears and emotions and societal expectations that cannot be discounted at play. So, you are happy that your ghost mom is making ghost friends, taking community college classes, doing all the things you know your mother could have done if things had been different.

Your ghost mom, still at the window giving chills to some kids playing on the sidewalk, says her ghost friend is going to be teaching a pottery class. She says she's excited at the prospect of sitting at the pottery wheel late into the night, dim lights and candles and *Unchained Melody*.

Then she pauses, letting that sink in.

You groan and roll your eyes.

Your ghost mom turns around and gives you a ghostly grin that's almost spine-chilling as a cat hisses on the sidewalk.

Visitation

You go to visit your mother's grave, and your
ghost mom comes along despite your protest.
She says that she wants to make sure her
tombstone is being kept clean, flowers being
freshened, candles lit. You don't really believe
her though, suspecting she has ulterior motives.
She was never one to care about such
formalities.

You both are standing at her grave.

Your ghost mom asks you if you remember
all the times she'd tell you—this during her
living life not her dead one—that one day you'd
be sorry when she was dead and gone. She
wants to know if you are sorry. Spring is nearly
ending and summer is coming on but it's an
unusually cold day for the time of year, so you
don't say anything and instead huddle in your
jacket. You can see the smirk on your ghost
mother's face, the pleasure of vindication—of
being right. And though your ghost mom is
dead, and you know that this, whatever it is,
can't last forever, that these moments may be the
last moments to say all the things you've wanted
to say, to forget the complicated, say things like
I love you or I'm sorry or tell her that sometimes
when you're alone and Gene Kelly comes on,
and he's twirling an umbrella, and it's raining,

and he's kicking up puddles, you call out *Mom come quick* before you remember that you don't have a mother anymore and quiet yourself. But you won't bring yourself to say these things.

You can't help wanting to deny your ghost mom the satisfaction.

About the Author

T Guzman is a writer living in southern
California. MFA graduate of Northern Michigan
University. Published in *Homology, Landlocked,
Press Pause Press,* and elsewhere.
Zebra Cakes connoisseur.
Exclamation point enthusiast.
Chicanx. He/him.